Usborne

Usborne
Sticker Dollies
Fairy Picnic

Zanna Davidson

Illustrated by Kat Uno

Cover illustration by Antonia Miller

Use the stickers to dress the Dollies on the "Meet the Dollies" pages

Meet the Magic Dollies

Lily, Holly and Grace are the "Magic Dollies."
They care for the magical creatures, from
unicorns to fairies and mermaids, that live
on the Enchanted Isle.

Lily

has a passion for
flowers and fairies. She is
brilliant at healing magical
creatures with her herbs
and flower potions.

★ Use the stickers to dress the Dollies ★

Holly

has a special relationship
with the trees and woodland
creatures in the Spellwoods.
She also loves the mermaids
that live by the Sparkling Shore.

Grace

is fascinated by all
magical creatures.
She reads books on how to
care for them and spends
as much time as she can
on the Enchanted Isle.

Dolly Town

The Magic Dollies live in Honeysuckle Cottage, in Dolly Town, home to all the Dollies. The Dollies work in teams to help those in trouble and are the very best at what they do, whether that's fashion design, ice skating or puppy training. Each day brings with it an exciting new adventure…

The **Shooting Star** train whisks the Dollies away on their missions.

Monique Coco's **Costume Emporium** has everything the Dollies might need.

The Dollies love to celebrate at the **Cupcake Café.**

Rose Theater

Animal Sanctuary

Bluebell Bookshop

Evergreen Sports Arena

Royal Palace

Palm Tree
Film Studios

Fashion Design
Studio

HEARTBEAT

Heartbeat
Dance Academy

Mission Control Center
lets the Dollies know
who's in trouble and
where to go.

Pop Star
Stadium

SPARKLES

Silver Sparkles
Skating Rink

Strawberry
Lane Stables

Honeysuckle Cottage
is home to the Magic Dollies.

Chapter One

Sparkle Dust

The Magic Dollies danced around their cottage in excitement. The fairies had invited them all to a picnic on the Enchanted Isle and, at last, the day of the picnic had arrived.

"I've been looking forward to
this for so long," said Lily. "All
the fairies are going to be there –

the Flower
Fairies...

and the
Tree Fairies...

the Sky
Fairies…

and the
Meadow
Fairies…"

"I know!" agreed Holly.

"I can't wait!"

Grace picked up the invitation
to take another look.

The Fairies invite
the **Magic Dollies**
to the **Spring Fairy Picnic**
on the Sparkling Shore.
Fairy Rose will meet you
at the entrance to the
Spellwoods at 2pm.

"Look!" said Lily, holding up their map of the Enchanted Isle. "The Sparkling Shore is right next to Mermaid Lagoon."

The Enchanted Isle

Fairy
Palace

Fairy
Ring

Silver Stream

Spellwoods

Pixie Meadows

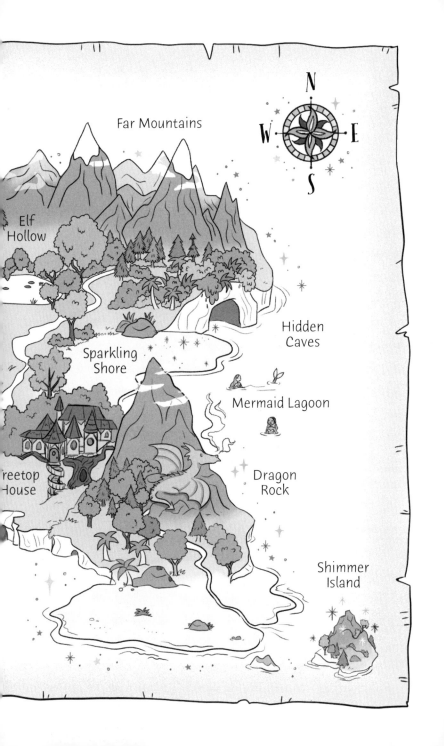

"Maybe we'll finally get to meet the mermaids!" said Holly.

I've read so much about them, but I've never *actually* seen one.

Just then, there was a whooshing sound and they all turned to see three little silver bags floating through the letter box.

"What's this?" wondered Grace. "Oh!" she said, picking up one of the bags. "There's a note. These are from the fairies. They've sent us tiny bags of sparkle dust."

Dear **Lily**, **Holly** and **Grace**,
Please sprinkle this over
yourselves when you arrive on
the Enchanted Isle. You're in
for a magical surprise!

"How exciting!" said Holly. "I
wonder what the sparkle dust is for?"

Lily checked her
watch. "Only
an hour until
we find out!"
she said.
"But first,

it's time for our appointment at Monique's Costume Emporium, so we can choose our outfits."

"It's such an honor to be invited to the picnic," added Holly. "I know Monique will help us look our best!"

The Dollies gathered their things and headed out across Dolly Town.

"What's in your bag, Lily?" asked Grace, noticing something sharp poking out of the side.

"Oh!" said Lily. "It's my magical potions book. I'm so used to taking it with me. Never mind. It'll just have to come to the Fairy Picnic!"

When they arrived at the Costume Emporium, the Magic Dollies headed straight to the famous glass elevator.

"Good afternoon, Magic Dollies," said Jasper, the elevator attendant. "You all look very excited."

"We're going to a Fairy Picnic," said Grace. "Take us to the Magical Department Floor please, Jasper."

We're all in need of very special clothes today.

The elevator whizzed up, before coming to a stop with a gentle

TING!

"I hope you find what you're looking for," said Jasper.

"Thank you," smiled Lily. "I'm sure we will!"

Chapter Two

Fairy Wings

The Magical Department Floor was filled with a soft green light, almost as if they'd stepped into an enchanted forest.

"Welcome," said Monique, gliding towards them. "What can I do for you today?"

"We'd love some clothes to wear to the Fairy Picnic," explained Lily. "I'm looking for a flowing dress embroidered with flowers."

"And what about you?" asked Monique, turning to Grace.

"Silver is my favorite color," said Grace, in her soft voice. "And I've been dreaming of sparkly shoes!"

"And I *love* clothes that are as green as the forest," said Holly.

Grace's clothes

A silver top

A silver star hair clip

A long silver skirt

Sparkly silver shoes

Lily's clothes

A flower garland

A flowing lilac dress, embroidered with flowers

Lilac shoes

Holly's clothes

A green, off-the-shoulder jumpsuit

An evergreen garland

A belt made of sorrel leaves

Soft green-felted slippers

Monique handed each
of the Magic Dollies their
clothes. Then their names
flashed up above the
changing rooms and
they stepped inside...

..."You all look
wonderful!" said Monique,
when they stepped out
again. "Perfect for a
Fairy Picnic."

30

Back on the warm, sunny street, Grace tapped the star symbol on her watch. A moment later, the glittering Shooting Star train drew up beside them.

"Good afternoon, Magic Dollies," said Sienna, the train driver, smiling at them from under her peaked cap.

"The Spellwoods on the Enchanted Isle, please," said Holly.

"Then step aboard," said Sienna. "I'll have you there in no time."

With a

WHOOSH

the train sped away. The Dollies
saw Dolly Town flash before their
eyes. Soon they were rushing
through a dark tunnel, twinkling
with tiny sparkly lights.

They shot out the other side, skimming over clear blue waters before the train finally drew to a halt where the woods ran down to the sea.

The Dollies stepped ashore and waved goodbye to Sienna, who sped away again in a sparkling cloud of dust.

"Isn't it beautiful!" said Holly, admiring the view. The sand on the beach was silky soft and behind them, the Spellwoods shone emerald green in the sunlight.

"I wonder if the unicorns will come to the picnic, too," said Grace, turning to Lily as she spoke. "I hope so."

But Lily was glancing down at her watch, a puzzled frown on her face. "It's two o'clock," she said. "Fairy Rose said she'd be here to greet us."

"I'm sure she'll be along soon," said Holly.

"But fairies are *never* late," Lily pointed out.

"You're right!" said Grace. "That does seem odd. What about the sparkle dust? Maybe we need to sprinkle it over ourselves first?"

They each opened up their little silver bag. "Ready?" said Lily. "Let's count to three!"

"One...two...three..." they chanted together, then sprinkled the sparkle dust over their heads.

Each of the Dollies shimmered for a moment in a pool of rainbow light. Then they began to shrink down...

down...

down...

One by one, they let out a gasp.

"Oh my goodness!" said Holly.

"I can't believe it!"

We're fairy-sized! And we've got... *wings!*

Chapter Three

Ogres!

For a moment, the Magic Dollies could only gaze at each other's wings in wonder. Then Holly began to flutter hers, lifting slightly from the ground.

"I'm flying!" she said. "Well, hovering…Let's see how high we can go!"

They flew up and up, sparkle dust glittering in the air around them. "WOW!" said Lily.

I've always wanted to be able to fly with the fairies.

But as they hovered in the warm air, there was still no sign of Fairy Rose. "What should we do now?" asked Grace. "Should we keep waiting for her? We really don't want to miss the picnic."

"I think we should go," said Holly. "Maybe Fairy Rose has been held up with all the planning?"

"And I've brought the map of the Enchanted Isle with me," added Lily, "so we'll be able to find our way."

She pulled the map out of her bag as she spoke. "Fairy Rose said to meet at the entrance to the Spellwoods, but the picnic is on the Sparkling Shore. All we need do is follow the Silver Stream. It looks as if it shouldn't take too long to get there."

The Dollies began
soaring over the treetops.
"The trees are like
giants!" said Holly.
"Isn't this magical?"
"It is!" agreed Lily.

"But I can't help feeling as
if something strange is
happening – and it's not
just being fairy-sized.
Do either of you
feel the same?"

"I suppose it's because everyone's at the picnic?" suggested Grace.

Lily shook her head. "It's not only that. I can't even hear any birdsong."

Just then, their watches began to flash.

"Mission Control here!" came a voice. "Are you there, Magic Dollies?"

"We're all here," said Grace, tapping her watch. "Has something happened?"

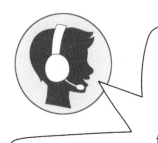

There's an
EMERGENCY on
the Enchanted Isle.
Three ogres have come
from their home beyond the
Far Mountains and are heading
towards the Sparkling Shore.
All the fairy creatures
are gathered there for the
Fairy Picnic.
If the ogres aren't stopped,
they'll destroy the Spellwoods
and crush the fairy creatures!

"Oh that's terrible!" gasped Grace. "Why are the ogres doing this?"

"Ogres are incredibly greedy," Lily pointed out. "Maybe they're coming for the food?"

"It's worse than that," explained Mission Control. "The ogres are furious they haven't been invited to the picnic. Last time the fairies asked them, they ate ALL the food and terrified the other guests. The fairies are doing everything they can to stop them, but nothing is working."

"Where are the ogres now?" asked Holly.

"We're sending through mission details and a map," said Mission Control. "It shows the ogres were last seen stampeding around the Fairy

Ring. But you'll have to hurry. The ogres are moving fast."

OGRES – IMPORTANT NOTES

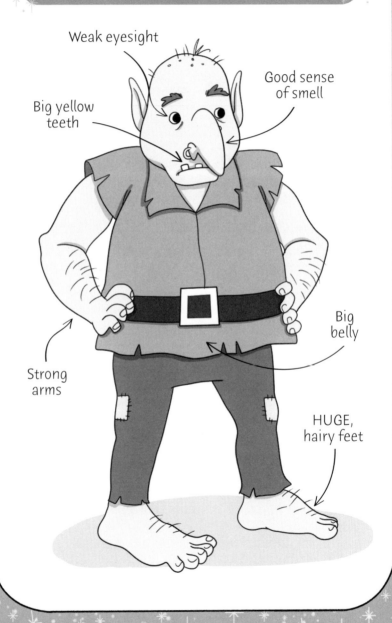

Weak eyesight

Good sense of smell

Big yellow teeth

Strong arms

Big belly

HUGE, hairy feet

"We're already on the Enchanted Isle," said Lily. "The fairies had invited us to the picnic. We're not too far from the Fairy Ring."

"Be careful," said Mission Control. "Those ogres can be dangerous."

"We know," replied Holly. "But we'll do whatever we can to help."

It's MISSION GO!

The Magic Dollies flew as fast as they could to the Fairy Ring. In the distance, they could hear the

THUMP! THUMP! THUMP!

of the ogres' footsteps and they could see the trees begin to quiver and shake. Then came their snorts and grunts and bellows.

"UGGHH!"
"GRRRR!"
"HURRUMPH!"

"There's one coming into view now!" said Grace, pointing.

The ogre was waving its huge fists in the air, trying to bat away a cloud of fairies.

The ogres would have looked
huge even if the Dollies were their
normal size, but now they
seemed like moving mountains.

"Look!" said Holly. "The
fairies are fighting back. They're
firing spells from the treetops!"

The spells shot across the sky
in beautiful arcs, sparkling and
crackling like fireworks.

But they didn't seem to make
any difference to the ogres, who

lumbered on, crashing through
the trees, making their way towards
the picnic spot by the sea.

"And there's Fairy Rose," said
Lily, pointing to a fairy, dressed
in pink, darting between the
branches. Lily waved to her and
Rose beckoned them over.

"Quick!" said Fairy Rose.
"Come and join me on this
branch. Then we can hide in
the tree while we talk."

"Mission Control told us
what was happening," said
Grace. "We've come to help."

Fairy Rose shook her head, almost
in despair. "Sorry I didn't come to
meet you. I wanted to fly with you
to the picnic. But then the ogres
came and I couldn't get away.

"None of the usual spells are
working! The fairy creatures are
already at the Sparkling Shore. They
can fly, but not very far or very well,
so they can't escape – not with the
ogres crashing through the trees.
It's too dangerous!"

"Has this ever happened before?" asked Lily.

"Never," said Fairy Rose. "We've always been able to stop the ogres. I don't understand what's going on."

"Could it be a problem with your wands?" asked Holly.

"I wondered that at first," said Fairy Rose. "But they can't *all* be broken. Look around! There are at least twenty fairies here, all firing out spells."

Then came a loud

CRASH

as an ogre stomped right past their tree. Up close, the Magic Dollies could see the ogre's thick, leathery skin and huge yellow teeth.

"They're destroying the Spellwoods," gasped Holly. "Look at all the trees that ogre has brought down."

"I know," said Fairy Rose. "And it'll be even worse if they reach the Sparkling Shore. With

the sea behind them, the fairy creatures will have nowhere to run. The ogres won't mean to hurt them, but they're so greedy, they'll just crush them in the rush for the food. What are we going to do?"

Chapter Four

A Cure for Sneezes

The Magic Dollies sat in thought for a moment, desperately trying to come up with a plan.

"What about your book on magical potions, Lily?" suggested Holly. "Is there anything in there that could help?"

Lily began leafing through the pages until she came to the chapter on ogres.

"It says here that, to ward off an ogre, the best spell you can use is the Stinkwort Spell. Apparently ogres can't stand the smell of it."

"That's the spell we're using," sighed Fairy Rose. "It's never failed us…until today."

At that moment, one of the ogres let out a loud sneeze. The force of it shook the branches of

the tree and they all had to cling
on, to stop themselves from being
blown away.

AAACHHOOOO!

Then another
ogre sneezed, and
another…

"It looks like one
of the fairies is trying
a sneezing spell!"
said Holly. "We'd
better take cover."

"I'm not so sure…"
said Fairy Rose, as
they sheltered
together under the
branches. "No one
would be using a

sneezing spell on the ogres. It's too dangerous! The force of their sneezes could be enough to blast down a whole tree."

"If it's not a spell, then the ogres must have colds," said Grace. "I really hope we don't get hit by ogre snot!"

"Hang on," said Lily, turning to Fairy Rose. "I've just thought of something…if the ogres have colds, could that explain why your Stinkwort Spells aren't working?"

"Yes, of course!" said Fairy Rose.

"That must be it. The spell wouldn't work if they can't smell! But I still don't know what to do. There's no other spell powerful enough to make the ogres turn around."

"Hang on," said Lily. "I'm sure there's a potion for this…" She flipped through the pages of her book. "Aha!" she said triumphantly. "Look at this!"

How to Cure an Ogre Cold

This recipe makes enough medicine for one ogre.

INGREDIENTS:

 Ten snarkle leaves, torn into pieces

Eight dream petals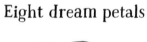

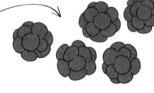 Three drops of silver birch sap

Five crushed dewberries

 Juice from a pixie apple

<u>STEP 1</u> - Pound all the ingredients, except the juice, into a mixture.

<u>STEP 2</u> - Add the juice from the pixie apple last of all, then stir.

<u>STEP 3</u> - Roll the mixture into a ball and feed to the ogre.

"Brilliant! There are three ogres, so we'll have to triple the amounts," said Fairy Rose. "But all the ingredients are right here in the Spellwoods. We'd better start looking right away."

"I'll let the fairies know what we're doing and keep a look out," said Grace.

I'll warn you if any ogres are coming our way.

"Lily, you're the best at making potions, should we bring the ingredients to you?" asked Holly.

Lily nodded in agreement. "Yes please," she said. "It's a shame I'm not in my potion room, but I'll do my best."

I can use sticks for stirring and a stone for pounding…

"Be as quick as you can!" called Grace, hovering above the treetops. "The ogres are starting to cross the Silver Stream. We haven't got much time."

Chapter Five
Battle
with the Ogres

Holly and Fairy Rose flew through the Spellwoods like the wind, gathering the ingredients for Lily's potion.

"This is the last
of the snarkle leaves
and dewberries,"
Holly called.
"I'll go and
look for the
pixie apples next."
"And I've got the
birch sap and
the dream
petals," said
Fairy Rose.

Lily worked as fast as she could, pounding and then stirring the mixture, before adding the juice from the pixie apples.

"How are we doing for time?" she called out to Grace, as she began shaping the mixture into balls.

"The fairies have managed to slow the ogres down with a freezing spell," Grace called back. "But each spell doesn't last long as the ogres are so big, and the poor fairies are exhausted. I don't know how much longer they can keep this up."

"Then we're just in time," said Lily, rolling the last of the mixture into a ball. "The cure for ogre colds is ready!"

"Wow!" said Fairy Rose. "Those look great."

"The tree sap binds them together," explained Lily. "That's how they keep their shape. They don't look very tasty though."

"Don't worry," said Fairy Rose.

Ogres will eat anything!

"Why don't you take one cold cure each?" suggested Fairy Rose. "The best plan is to fly fast towards the ogres, then throw the cold cures at them at the last moment. With luck, the ogres will gobble them up. I'll let the other fairies know the plan."

Lily handed out the cold cures to Holly and Grace.

Then they fluttered their wings once more and flew high above the treetops, chasing after the ogres.

"Oh no!" called Grace. "The ogres are very nearly at the Sparkling Shore."

The fairy rabbits were anxiously hopping between the shoreline and back.

"Please stop the ogres!" squeaked the fairy hedgehogs. "Our wings are too small for us to fly past them."

"Don't worry," Fairy Rose called back. "We have a plan."

The other fairies flew overhead, so they were hovering above the fairy creatures, calling down to reassure them.

"Good luck, Magic Dollies," said Fairy Rose.

"We won't fail," said Holly,
determinedly. She turned to the
Magic Dollies. "Are you ready?
Let's take on these ogres!"

Lily and Grace waited until they were close enough, then threw the medicine balls, one at each ogre, aiming straight for their mouths.

As if mesmerized, both ogres watched the medicine balls flying towards them, then opened their gaping mouths…and swallowed them down!

"Two ogres down!" called Lily.

Holly took aim at the last ogre, flying in even closer, determined to succeed. Up close, she could see the strange green sheen of his skin and smell his musty breath.

She pulled back her arm, then flung her medicine ball into the air.

But at that moment,
the ogre turned his head
away and Holly let out a cry
of concern as the ball began
to drop towards the ground.
"Oh no!" thought Holly.
"It's not going to work…"

Then, at the last moment, the ogre caught the medicine ball in his great fist, popped it into his mouth and gulped it down.

With a cry of relief, Holly
turned to see the others
cheering and hugging
in celebration.

Hooray!
We've
done it!

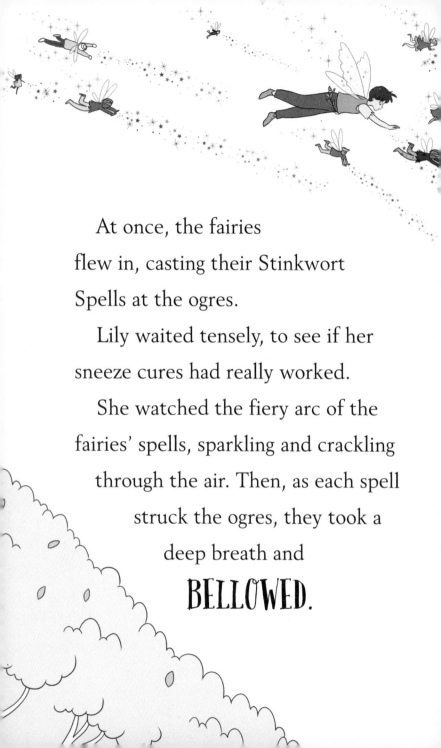

At once, the fairies
flew in, casting their Stinkwort
Spells at the ogres.

Lily waited tensely, to see if her
sneeze cures had really worked.

She watched the fiery arc of the
fairies' spells, sparkling and crackling
through the air. Then, as each spell
struck the ogres, they took a
deep breath and

BELLOWED.

They turned and ran back
through the Spellwoods so that it
thundered with the sound of ogre
footsteps. These became fainter
and fainter as the ogres
disappeared into the mountains.

"Hooray!" cried Holly. "We've defeated the ogres!"

She looked down to see all the fairy creatures rejoicing on the beach, dancing and laughing.

Grace tapped the Mission Control symbol on her watch. "Mission Control!" she said. "Are you there?"

"We're here," said Mission Control. "Is everything okay?"

"Mission complete," said Grace, smiling.

"We hear you," said Mission Control.

"Congratulations, Magic Dollies. Now you can enjoy the picnic!"

"There's just one problem," said Lily, ruefully, looking down at the Sparkling Shore.

"What is it?" asked Grace.

"Look!" said Lily. "The picnic… it's in ruins! It's been scattered across the beach by the ogres' sneezes!"

Chapter Six

The Sparkling Shore

The Dollies gazed at what was left of the picnic. Baskets had been blown over, the blankets had been blasted away and little fairy cakes were bobbing out to sea.

"Oh what a shame," said Holly. When they saw what had happened, the fairy hedgehogs

started sniffling, and the rabbits began to cry.

Fairy Rose flew high above them all. "Let's rescue what we can! Flower Fairies, search for the blankets! Tree Fairies, see if you can find the picnic baskets. Sky and Meadow Fairies – gather all the food you can find, even if it's wet and sandy."

In a flutter of shimmering wings, the fairies flew up and down the beach and over the frothing waves, gathering all the pieces of the picnic. Then they laid them out on the ground beneath Fairy Rose.

"It still looks a very sorry sight," said Holly, taking in the sand-covered blankets and soggy cakes.

"Aha!" said Fairy Rose. "That's what **magic** is for!"

She waved her wand over the picnic and chanted a spell beneath her breath. At once, the air was filled with rainbow sparkles. When they cleared, all the fairy creatures gave a great cheer. The blankets

shook themselves free of sand and
settled in a circle on the beach.
The picnic baskets opened up
their lids and out came the plates,
shiny and clean, floating through
the air before coming to
settle on the blankets.

As for the food…

"WOW!" said Grace.

"Time to feast!" said Fairy Rose.

The Magic Dollies sat down on the blankets; the fairy rabbits nibbled on the tasty flowers, while the fairy mice couldn't resist the cakes and pastries.

Then one of the fairies pulled out a silver flute and began to play a beautiful tune.

"It's to let the mermaids know it's safe to come," explained Fairy Rose. "And the unicorns too. They're both very shy though, so they don't always join us."

"I hope they do," murmured Grace, looking expectantly into the Spellwoods.

Then out came two unicorns – a mother and a foal. "Look!" said Grace. "Here are the unicorns we helped the last time we visited."

"And I can see a mermaid too!" said Holly, gazing out at the sea. "I'm so excited."

One by one, the mermaids rose to the surface, casting dancing ripples across the water.

"Can we go over and say hello?" asked Holly.

But Fairy Rose shook her head. "The mermaids are very shy and private," she said. "You don't want to scare them. Try waiting for a mermaid to approach you first."

Holly watched the mermaids for a while, as they sat combing their hair on the rocks. Then her attention was caught by the sound of fairy music. She went to sit with the other Magic Dollies, feasting and listening to the music until the sun set across the sea.

"We'd best be going home now," said Lily. "Thank you so much for inviting us to the picnic."

"Thank you for helping us fight the ogres," said Fairy Rose.

We couldn't have done it without you.

We were so glad to be able to help.

Grace said a last goodbye to the unicorns, while Holly headed down to the shore, to gaze at the mermaids one final time. To her delight, one of the mermaids on the rocks waved to her, then dived into the sea. She rose up again, not far from Holly, and gave her a brief, beautiful smile,

before disappearing beneath the waves.

Fairy Rose fluttered over to Holly's side. "It's rare to receive a mermaid's smile on first meeting," she said. "I think you must have a special connection with them."

"I hope so," said Holly. "I'll always treasure that moment."

Then, with a final wave, the
Magic Dollies took to the air, flying
over the Spellwoods.

When the Magic Dollies touched
down on the far shore, the last of
the light left the sky. Holly could
feel herself growing and stretching,
back to her normal size.

She looked over her shoulder,
just in time to see her wings
disappear in a cloud of sparkle dust.

Oh! Our wings…

"They've gone!" said Lily. "I knew they would…But wasn't it magical, being able to fly?"

"It was," agreed Grace. "I hope we can do it again someday."

Then she tapped the star symbol on her watch, to summon the Shooting Star train.

It soon drew up beside them in a cloud of glittering stars.

"Hello, Magic Dollies," said

Sienna, smiling at them. "How was the picnic?"

"Eventful!" laughed Lily. "We saw unicorns and mermaids and ate the most delicious fairy food…but we also had to fight off a few ogres!"

"And where would you like to go now?" asked Sienna. "You usually end your missions at the Cupcake Café, but I expect you're too full after the picnic for that."

Holly looked at the others and then grinned, knowing exactly what they were thinking. "Cupcake Café it is!" she said. "No mission is complete without a hot chocolate at the end."

"With marshmallows on top," added Grace.

"And whipped cream…" laughed Lily.

"In that case, climb aboard!" said Sienna.

The Shooting Star train whooshed away from the Enchanted Isle, through the tunnel sparkling with stars, before winding its way through Dolly Town.

By the time they drew up outside the Cupcake Café it was dark, and the moon hung huge and silver in the sky.

The Dollies waved goodbye and stepped inside the café, heading for their favorite cozy corner at the back.

"The usual, please, Maya," said Lily, smiling at the owner of the Cupcake Café. "We've had a busy afternoon battling ogres!"

"Enjoy!" said Maya, when she brought over the hot chocolates. "It sounds like you've earned them."

"Thank you, Maya," replied Grace. "These look *perfect*."

As they sipped their creamy hot chocolates, each of the Dollies was quiet for a moment, thinking over the excitement of the day. "I do hope we can go back to the Enchanted Isle again soon," said Lily.

"Me too," said Grace. "It was lovely to see the unicorns again."

"And to meet the mermaids," added Holly. "Hopefully, from now on, they'll call on us whenever they're in trouble."

"But for now, we can celebrate the end of another successful mission," said Lily.

The Magic Dollies put their arms around each other and grinned. "Magic Dollies forever!" they chanted.

The End

Join the **Magic Dollies**
on their other adventures.

Visit usbornebooksandmore.com
or edcpub.com to see more in
this series.